HEiDi HECKELBECK
and the Hair Emergency!

By Wanda Coven
Illustrated by Priscilla Burris

LITTLE SIMON

New York London Toronto Sydney New Delhi

LITTLE SIMON
An imprint of Simon & Schuster Children's Publishing Division
1230 Avenue of the Americas, New York, New York 10020
First Little Simon hardcover edition December 2020
Copyright © 2020 by Simon & Schuster, Inc.
Also available in a Little Simon paperback edition.
All rights reserved, including the right of reproduction in whole or in part in any form. LITTLE SIMON is a registered trademark of Simon & Schuster, Inc., and associated colophon is a trademark of Simon & Schuster, Inc. For information about special discounts for bulk purchases, please contact Simon & Schuster Special Sales at 1-866-506-1949 or business@simonandschuster.com.
The Simon & Schuster Speakers Bureau can bring authors to your live event. For more information or to book an event contact the Simon & Schuster Speakers Bureau at 1-866-248-3049 or visit our website at www.simonspeakers.com.
Designed by Ciara Gay
Manufactured in the United States of America 1020 FFG
10 9 8 7 6 5 4 3 2 1
This book has been cataloged with the Library of Congress.
ISBN 978-1-5344-8578-5 (hc)
ISBN 978-1-5344-8577-8 (pbk)
ISBN 978-1-5344-8579-2 (ebook)

CONTENTS

Chapter 1

THE ROLY-POLY PUPPY

Heidi snuggled under a blanket with her new book, *Jolly Roger, the Pirate Puppy*. This little hound sailed the seven seas on the hunt for buried treasure. Heidi wondered what it would be like to sail with a pirate puppy and dig up treasure.

Then Heidi heard a shriek of laughter and dropped her book on the floor. She sat up on the sofa and looked around. *HENRY!*

Heidi shouted in her best pirate voice, "Aaargh! What be the problem, little brother?"

Henry paid no attention to his sister. He was too busy chasing something around the family room.

Heidi rolled onto her side to see what it was. Henry's new windup toy—the Roly-Poly Puppy—sped and spun around in circles. This puppy had wheels instead of stubby puppy legs . . . and it was fast.

Henry picked the puppy up and set
it down on the floor. He pulled back
on the string to wind up the wheels.
Then Henry let the toy go.

That Roly-Poly Puppy zoomed all over the carpet. Plus, every time it bumped into something, it giggled, turned around, and took off again in another direction.

"*Bonk!*" It bumped into the leg of a chair. "*Hee-hee! Heedle! Heedle! Hee!*"

Then the toy turned and charged into the game cabinet. "*Bonk! Hee-hee! Heedle! Heedle! Hee!*"

Henry laughed, squealed, and chased after the puppy again and again. Heidi sighed. Then she picked up her book and tried to get back into her reading. But it was impossible. All she could hear was *"Bonk! Hee-hee! Heedle! Heedle! Hee!"*

Heidi snapped her book shut just as Dad walked into the room. He went right over to Henry.

Now Henry's gonna GET IT, Heidi thought.

But her little brother didn't get in trouble. Instead, Dad said, "Hey, buddy. Do you want to taste-test my soda? It's dill pickle flavored!"

Henry stopped chasing his Roly-Poly Puppy. He never turned down a chance to help Dad. Plus, he loved dill pickles.

"Sure!" Henry cheered. "Can Roly-Poly Puppy try it too?"

Dad shook his head. "Sorry, champ. Windup toys are *not* allowed near my experiments. You can leave him here."

Henry set the Roly-Poly Puppy on the side table next to Heidi. He waggled a finger at his sister.

"No touching!" he warned her in a baby voice that annoyed Heidi to no end.

"As if!" she said, laying her head on the arm of the sofa.

With that, Henry followed Dad to the basement.

"Finally some peace and quiet!" Heidi said to the empty room.

But as soon as Heidi uttered those words, the Roly-Poly Puppy let out a very evil giggle and zoomed off the table . . . right onto Heidi's head!

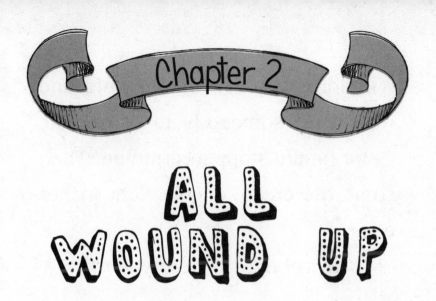

Chapter 2

ALL WOUND UP

"Aaaaaaaaaaah!" Heidi screamed, her shoulders tightening.

She felt the gears on the Roly-Poly Puppy catch in her hair. They grew tighter and tighter on her scalp.

"HELP! Henry's toy is EATING my hair!" she shouted.

Heidi lay frozen on the sofa and waited for somebody to come. The gears finally stopped grinding. Then came the creepy giggle right in her ear.

"Hee-hee! Heedle! Heedle! Hee!"

Heidi yelled again. "SOMEBODY, HELP ME!"

Finally she heard Dad's footsteps thumping up the basement stairs and Mom's flats tapping across the floor. Everyone arrived at the same time.

"My HAIR . . . !" Heidi wailed, pointing at the toy stuck to the side of her head.

"My PUPPY!" Henry shouted.

"My GOODNESS!" said Mom. "Now, everybody, stay *calm*."

Mom reached in and tried to gently separate the toy puppy from Heidi's hair. But the toy didn't budge.

"OW!" Heidi yelped.

"What if we pour olive oil on top of her head?" Henry suggested. "The oil might make the puppy slide off more easily."

Heidi glared at her brother. "Are you KIDDING ME?"

Henry quickly hid behind Dad.

"Actually, Henry's idea may work," said Dad.

Heidi sighed loudly. "But I don't want OLIVE OIL in my hair! It sounds GROSS. Can't we just take Henry's stupid toy APART?"

Henry jumped out from behind Dad. "Wait! You can't do that!" he cried. "That is my FAVORITE toy ever!"

Mom groaned. "It is really stuck in there, Heidi. Let's give it a try."

"Okay, *OKAY!*" she said. "Try the dumb oil—just get this thing out of my hair!"

Dad hurried to the kitchen and grabbed a bottle of olive oil. Then he poured a little on the wheels of the Roly-Poly Puppy. He gently tugged on the toy, being careful not to pull Heidi's hair.

"Is it working?" she asked.

"A little," Dad said. "But your hair is really caught in there."

Heidi squeezed her eyes shut and wailed, "OUCH! You're making it worse!"

Mom patted Heidi on the shoulder. "I have an idea," she said, "but you might not like it."

"Mom, I don't care WHAT you do,"
Heidi whimpered. "Just PA-LEEZE get
this toy out of my hair!"

Mom raced to her office and came back with a pair of scissors and a comb. She stood behind Heidi, found where the toy was stuck, and slid the scissors in between the toy and Heidi's scalp.

Snip!

Mom cut the Roly-Poly Puppy from
Heidi's hair and handed it to Henry.

"You're free!" Dad cheered.

Heidi sat up and touched the side
of her head. The Roly-Poly Puppy

was gone! Still, something didn't feel quite right.

Hmm, has my hair always been this short? Heidi wondered.

Then her eyes grew wide.

"Mom," Heidi whispered, "what did you do to my HAIR?"

Chapter 3

MOP CHOP

Heidi looked at the scissors in Mom's hand. Mom quickly hid them behind her back.

"Don't panic, Heidi," Mom said nervously. "I trimmed off a little more than I thought, but I'll fix it. I promise!"

Mom picked up the comb and ran it through Heidi's hair. She tried to hide the *missing* hair with the remaining hair. But no matter how much she combed, it didn't work.

"We need professional help," Mom declared. "I'm going to take you to the salon."

Heidi covered her head with a sofa pillow. "Does the salon have an emergency room?" she asked. "Because this is a huge HAIR EMERGENCY."

Henry held out Heidi's missing hair, which he had just finished yanking from the wheels of his Roly-Poly Puppy. "Maybe they can perform surgery and reattach this," he suggested.

Heidi stared in horror at her shorn hair. Her eyes filled with tears.

"Let's go," said Mom gently. She handed Heidi a jacket, and they headed to the car.

Heidi sat with her head below the window. She didn't want anyone to see her ugly hair. When they arrived at the salon, Heidi draped her jacket over her head to get from the car into the salon. She left it on in the waiting area, too.

"Heidi?" called a stylist. Heidi walked to the stylist's chair and sat down. Mom followed.

"What can I do for you?" the stylist asked.

Heidi pulled her jacket off her head while Mom explained what had happened. The stylist played with Heidi's hair for a minute or two.

"Well, I have some good news and some *maybe* good news," the stylist said. She pumped the lever on the chair, and Heidi went up, up, up. Normally, Heidi loved salon chairs but not today. She waited for the stylist to explain her options.

"The good news is that I can fix your hair," said the stylist. "The *maybe* good news is that it would have to be a *very* short haircut."

Heidi looked at the stylist in the mirror. "HOW short?"

The stylist held up electric clippers and turned them on. The sudden clack and angry buzz from the clippers shocked Heidi as she jolted in her seat.

"NO, thank you!" she said, slipping out of the chair. She grabbed Mom by the hand and led her out the door.

"This hair emergency is totally HOPELESS," Heidi complained once they were back in the car.

"Maybe the salon wasn't the best idea, but don't worry," said Mom. "I have a *plan*."

Chapter 4

A NEW DO

Mom drove straight to Aunt Trudy's house and parked in the driveway. Heidi popped up in her seat and looked out the window with a smile. Aunt Trudy was the most experienced witch in the family, and if anyone could help fix this mess, it was her.

"Good thinking, Mom!" Heidi exclaimed.

She hopped out of the car without waiting for Mom and ran up the front walk to ring the doorbell.

Oh, please be home! Heidi thought.

Aunt Trudy opened the door, and when she saw Heidi, she clasped her hands together. "What a wonderful surprise!" exclaimed her aunt, who had red hair like Heidi. Aunt Trudy wore her hair in a single braid down her back. "What's the occasion?"

Heidi hung her head. "I have a big problem," she said, pointing to the bald patch in her hair.

"Oh my! Come in and tell me what happened," Aunt Trudy said. "I'm sure it's an exciting story."

Heidi and Mom
took turns telling
Aunt Trudy about
the hair-eating
Roly-Poly Puppy.
Aunt Trudy pressed
her fingers to her lips
and giggled.

"Please don't laugh," Heidi said,
covering her head with
her hand. "Nobody's
been able to fix it—
not even the lady
at the salon. You're
my ONLY hope!"

"I'm sorry," Aunt Trudy said gently. "I completely understand. The reason I laughed was because your mother used to play hairdresser on her dolls when we were little. And *now* she's playing hairdresser on her own daughter!"

Mom rolled her eyes. "This may not be the best time to bring that up, Trudy."

But Heidi actually smiled. She imagined all her mother's dolls with bad haircuts.

"Now follow me into the kitchen, and let's see what we can do about this," said Aunt Trudy.

She pulled her own *Book of Spells* from the shelf and thumbed through the pages.

For the first time all day, Heidi began to feel hopeful.

"Let's see, we have split ends, cowlicks, baldness . . . Oh, here we go," said Aunt Trudy as she settled on a spell called A New Do. "Oh my, this is *very* interesting. This spell actually requires *three* witches to perform it."

Aunt Trudy laid the *Book of Spells* on the kitchen table so they could all read it together.

A New Do

Are you having a bad hair day? Perhaps you got a wad of gum stuck in your locks. Or maybe you just got a bad haircut. If you're in need of a new do, then this is the spell for you!

Ingredients:

1 strand of hair

1 hairbrush

3 squirts of detangler

1 piece of gingerroot

Stir the ingredients together in a mixing bowl. Have one witch hold her Witches of Westwick medallion over her heart. Then all three witches must chant the following spell together.

HAiR, DiDDLE DOO! HAiR, DOODLE DEE!

REPAiR _____'s hAiR,

[PERSON'S NAME]

ON THE COUNT OF THREE.

ONE! TWO! THREE!

Heidi and Mom helped Aunt Trudy collect the ingredients. Heidi grabbed detangler from the bathroom. Aunt Trudy found an old hairbrush in her purse. And Mom pulled a piece of gingerroot from the fridge.

Heidi plucked a hair from her head and dropped it into the bowl. Mom added a strand of her hair too.

"But, Mom, I already added a piece of hair," said Heidi.

Mom looked at Heidi and Aunt Trudy. "Oh, I thought each of us had to add a strand of hair since it takes three witches to cast the spell."

Aunt Trudy looked in the bowl. "I believe we only needed a piece of hair from the patient."

Mom frowned. "Oh dear! Should we start over?"

Aunt Trudy just shook her head. "I don't have another gingerroot to start over with, but no worries! It should be fine."

Heidi watched as Aunt Trudy hung her medallion around her neck and held it over her heart. Then the three Witches of Westwick chanted the spell.

Swoosh! Sparkles swirled from the bowl, and Heidi felt a tingling sensation on her scalp. She ran her hands through her hair.

"My hair is BACK!" she cried.

Chapter 5

HAiR SHE IS!

When Heidi woke up the next morning, the first thing she did was check her hair in the mirror. Luckily, it was all there. Plus, it shined like it had just been washed and styled.

Heidi flipped her hair as if she were in a shampoo commercial.

My hair looks AMAZING, she thought.

And hair this amazing needed the perfect outfit. Heidi picked out her clothes, got dressed, and zipped downstairs for breakfast.

Henry was already slurping his banana-strawberry smoothie. Mom placed a bowl of oatmeal with cinnamon apple slices in front of Heidi. It smelled spice-o-licious.

"Well, here she is!" Mom announced. "Or, dare I say, HAIR she is!"

Dad set a stack of clean cereal bowls on the shelf and looked at Heidi. "Wow! Your hair looks as good as new!"

Heidi picked up her spoon and dug into her oatmeal. "Thanks!" she said before taking a big bite.

Mom turned around and started on the breakfast dishes while Dad emptied the silverware from the dishwasher. Everything was back to normal until Henry set down his smoothie and stared at his sister. His mouth fell open.

"What's YOUR problem?" Heidi
asked.

"Your HAIR," Henry whispered. "It
looks like MOM'S hair."

Heidi dropped her spoon in her bowl. Then she pushed back her chair and ran to the mirror beside the back door. But Henry must have been teasing her, because her hair looked totally normal now.

"Dad, Henry's being mean," Heidi said as she walked back to the table.

Dad turned around. "Be nice to your sister, Henry," he said, and gave Heidi a nod. She began to eat her oatmeal again, but Henry kept staring at her.

"What now?" Heidi asked in a huff. "Let me guess, I've got Dad's hair?"

"Actually," Henry began . . . because she *did* have Dad's hair.

Then Heidi's hair changed into HENRY'S hairstyle right before his eyes!

"Uh, may I please be excused, Mom?" Henry asked. "I don't feel very well."

Heidi jumped up to check her hair in the mirror, but it was normal.

Meanwhile, Mom hurried to the table and felt Henry's forehead.

"Well, you're not warm," she said. "I'm sure you'll feel better once you get outside."

"I hope so," Henry said as he grabbed his backpack and raced out the door without looking at his sister.

Dad chuckled. "He seems fine to me."

"And you'd better get going too, Heidi," Mom said.

Heidi took a last bite of oatmeal, then checked her hair in the mirror one more time before she left for the day. She smiled at her reflection.

This is going to be a GREAT hair day! she thought.

Chapter 6

JELLYFiSH HAiR

Heidi sat next to Bruce Bickerson on the bus. She pulled out her Pirate Puppy book and opened it to her bookmark.

"Sorry, I can't talk today," Heidi said, not looking up. "I have to finish my reading homework."

Heidi's hair emergency had taken up all her reading time.

"That's okay," Bruce said. Then he noticed Heidi's shiny hair. "Wow! Your hair is shimmering like a jellyfish."

Heidi laughed, because only Bruce would give such a scientific compliment.

"Thanks," she said, not looking up from her book. "My aunt gave me a special hair treatment."

The bus drove along through the neighborhood. At the next stop, Heidi glanced at Bruce, who was looking out the window. Then she noticed her reflection in the windowpane. Instead of her own hair, she had Bruce's hair on top of her head!

"Eek!" Heidi squeaked, and quickly covered her head with her book.

Bruce flinched and turned to stare at his friend. "What are you doing?"

Heidi had to think fast. "Uh, did you see a pirate OVER THERE?" Heidi pointed to the other side of the bus.

Bruce turned to look, which gave Heidi time to check her reflection in the window again. This time her hair was back to normal.

"A pirate on our bus?" Bruce asked. "What are you even talking about?"

Heidi laughed nervously. "Oh, silly me! The pirate is in my BOOK—not on the bus! I must have, um, gotten caught up in the story."

Heidi didn't dare look up the whole time she was talking. She had a funny feeling that if she looked at Bruce, her hair would change again.

"Something weird is going on," Bruce said. "Are you okay?"

Heidi pretended to laugh it off. But Bruce was right—something weird *was* going on. Her hair emergency had just gotten so much worse.

Chapter 7

OCTOPUS HAIR

Heidi kept her nose in her book the rest of the way to school. Then she waited for everyone to get off the bus—even Bruce. And all those kids took a long time to leave.

Maybe I just IMAGINED myself with Bruce's hair, Heidi thought.

But then she remembered what Henry had said at breakfast. *Your HAIR. It looks like MOM'S hair.*

Suddenly Heidi's eyes grew wide. She realized that Aunt Trudy's spell must have gone wrong.

But what triggers my hair to change? she wondered. *Is it my moods? Or does it only happen when I say certain words?*

As Heidi thought, she looked out the window and noticed Stanley Stonewrecker talking to Melanie Maplethorpe on the playground. Stanley saw Heidi and waved. As soon as Heidi saw Stanley, her scalp began to tingle. . . . *Uh-oh*, she thought.

Heidi put her hand on her head. This time she could *feel* her hair changing. And now it felt short, like Stanley's haircut. She quickly slunk down in her seat. *Okay, now I get it!* she said to herself. *If I look at somebody, I get THAT person's hairstyle.*

"Please exit the bus!" the driver
said.

Heidi knew the bus driver was
talking to her. She slowly stood up
and checked her bewitched hair in
the rearview mirror. It had gone back
to normal.

Now she needed to find a place to hide. This way, no one would see her hair change.

With her eyes fixed on the ground, Heidi charged down the stairs of the bus. She sprinted across the playground and into the school. Then she zoomed straight to the girls' room and locked herself in a stall.

Heidi caught her breath and hatched a plan. If she could get to the nurse's office, then she could call her mom. She just needed to wait until the coast was clear. The thought of walking through a crowded hallway made Heidi's magic hair shiver.

She listened until the noise outside quieted down, and then she opened the stall to leave . . . just as Melanie walked into the bathroom with Bryce Beltran and Natalie Newman.

Heidi stepped back into the stall and latched the door, but it was too late. Heidi had seen all three girls.

Her scalp started to tingle as her hair twisted and twirled. It reached out like the tentacles of an octopus.

Heidi tried to control her hair with her hands, but it was no use. Her magic hair had a mind of its own.

Thankfully, Heidi stayed hidden inside the stall. She kept very still and hoped nobody could see through the cracks.

Her classmates talked until the bell rang. Then they shuffled back into the hallway.

Heidi quickly unlatched the door and looked at herself in the mirror. Her hair was back to normal again.

Without waiting another second, Heidi took a deep breath and *bolted* for the nurse's office.

Chapter 8

GETAWAY GIRL

Heidi kept her head down and walked as fast as she could without running. She was trying to look as normal as possible. Out of the corner of her eye she watched for the water fountain. The nurse's office was one door *after* the water fountain.

"Well, if it isn't my wonder twin!" Mrs. Foster exclaimed.

Mrs. Foster was the school nurse, and she had the exact same hairstyle and hair color as Heidi. The best part of being twins today was that Heidi's hairstyle didn't change when she looked at Mrs. Foster.

"Are you feeling okay?" asked Mrs. Foster.

Heidi shook her head. "No. May I please call my mom?"

Mrs. Foster handed her phone to Heidi. "Of course you may," she said reassuringly.

Heidi called her mom and told her she was feeling a little "hairy." Mom knew that was code for "something went wrong with the spell." She said she would be right over.

Heidi sat on the cot and waited for what seemed like *forever*.

Then she heard her mother's voice. Mom came over and took Heidi by the hand. Heidi was careful not to look at Mom. They thanked Mrs. Foster and quickly departed.

On the way to the car, Heidi told Mom how her hair changed styles whenever she looked at people.

"Oh my!" her mother gasped. "Then you'd better not look at anyone!"

Heidi sighed. "I'm doing my best."

As they hopped in the getaway car, Heidi heard Principal Pennypacker's voice in the distance.

"Hope you feel better, Heidi!" he called from the top of the stairs. Without thinking, Heidi looked at the principal.

"Thanks!" she said. Then . . .
WHAMMO!

Heidi's hair turned into PRINCIPAL
PENNYPACKER'S HAIR!

Heidi yelped and slid down in her
seat. "Cover for me!"

Mom smiled nervously at the
principal and hit the gas.

"Did he see anything?" Heidi asked.

Mom snuck a glance in the mirror. She could see the principal scratching his head.

"He looks very confused," said Mom, "but we can't worry about that right now. We have to fix your hair."

Heidi sat up in her seat. "Are we going back to Aunt Trudy's?"

Mom shook her head. "No, she's working. I'm afraid this time we're on our own."

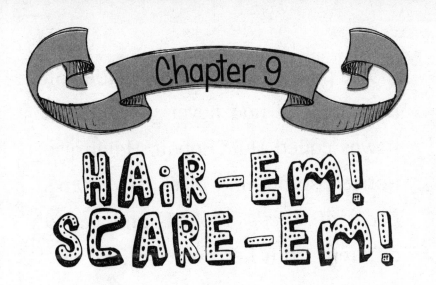

Chapter 9

HAiR-EM! SCARE-EM!

Mom pulled out her *Book of Spells* from the window seat in her office. Her spell book was white with gold lettering. She dusted off the cover and set the book on her desk. The book opened, and the pages began to turn on their own.

The pages fluttered, then settled on a spell Heidi had never seen before. It was called Hair Repair. Heidi also noticed something else: Her mom's *Book of Spells* looked and acted different from her own.

"How come the pages in my *Book of Spells* don't turn by themselves?" Heidi asked. "And why does your spell book have different spells? Our books aren't even the same color!"

"Well," Mom began, "all Witches and Wizards of Westwick have their own unique *Book of Spells*. Each book has its own look and works in its own special way. *My* book is perfectly suited to *me*—just as *your* book is perfectly suited to *you*."

Heidi thought that sounded cool. "That means we're both special!"

"It most certainly does!" Mom said with a smile. Then she circled the spell with her finger. "Now let's focus on fixing your hair so you can be *your* own perfect self again too."

Heidi and Mom read over the spell together.

Hair Repair

Do you have unruly hair? A bad dye job? Perhaps your hair has a mind of its own. Or did you perform a hair spell that went wrong? If you're in need of some hair repair, then this is the spell for you!

Ingredients:

1 regular pencil

1 regular blank sheet of paper

2 regular thumbtacks

1 regular glass of milk

Mix the ingredients together in a bowl. Two witches must each hold their Witches of Westwick medallions in one hand and place their other hand over the mix. Chant the following spell together:

HAIR-EM! SCARE-EM!

BAD hair, BEWARE!

SALON chair! BARBER chair!

REPAIR My hair!

Heidi and Mom collected all the
ingredients in a mixing bowl. Then
they each held a medallion in one
hand and placed the other hand over
the mix before they chanted the spell.

Bright sparkles swirled from the bowl and circled all around Heidi's head—just as the first spell had done.

Heidi's hair began to transform. It cycled through all the new hairstyles she'd had that day in reverse: *Principal Pennypacker's hair. The hair from the girls in the girls' room. Stanley's hair. Bruce's hair. Henry's hair. Dad's hair. And Mom's hair.*

Finally, Heidi got her very own head of hair back. Except there was still one little problem.

Chapter 10

A NEW LOOK

Heidi was excited until she looked in the mirror and moaned.

The hair that got cut off in the Roly-Poly Puppy disaster was missing all over again.

"I'm right back to where I started!" Heidi whimpered.

Mom looked deep in thought. Then her face lit up.

"I have an idea!" she said, and she ran upstairs to her room.

Heidi could hear the crinkle of a shopping bag followed by Mom trotting back downstairs.

Mom stood in front of Heidi with both hands behind her back. "Which hand?"

Heidi pointed to Mom's right hand. Mom handed Heidi a heart-shaped hand mirror. She still had one hand behind her back.

"*Now* which hand?"

Heidi pointed to Mom's left hand. This time Mom handed her daughter a wide, star-studded headband.

Heidi squealed. "For ME?"

Mom nodded. "I was saving these for your Valentine's Day gift, but it seems like you might need them earlier."

Heidi set down the mirror and pushed the headband through her hair. She picked up the mirror and looked at herself.

"Look! It perfectly
covers my missing
hair!" she cheered.

Mom clapped
her hands. "It
sure does!"

Heidi looked at
her hair from all
sides in the mirror.
The stars sparkled as
she moved.

"I love it so much!"
she exclaimed. "This
headband is positively MAGICAL."

Mom raised an eyebrow.

"Not in a witchy way, of course!"
Heidi added.

Then both Mom and Heidi burst
out laughing.

Check out the next book starring

HEiDi HECKELBECK

Surprise!

Surprise!

SURPRISE!

Aunt Trudy had a big surprise for Heidi and Henry Heckelbeck. She was taking them to the Brewster Library for the town's Reading Party celebration. There were going to be authors, illustrators, and more at the

An excerpt from *Heidi Heckelbeck and the Lost Library Book*

and Heidi couldn't wait!

p in!" cried Aunt Trudy as she
d the car door.

Heidi and Henry scrambled
back seat and buckled their
ts.

laid her shoulder bag on
She liked to take her bag on
outings. It made her feel very
up.

y had brought a bag too—his
. It had a magnifying glass, a
k, and a pen inside.

glared at her brother. "Oh no,
ot in SPY mode, are you?"

i Heckelbeck and the Lost Library Book

Henry held up the magni[...]
glass and winked at his sister[...]
ALWAYS in spy mode!"

Heidi rolled her eyes.

"Well, I'm in spy mode too[...]
Trudy said as she pulled out[...]
driveway. "And right now, I s[...]
mom waving good-bye."

Aunt Trudy waved at Mom. [...]
did too.

Heidi sighed and looked o[...]
window. She spied two so[...]
playing tag, but she kept[...]
information to herself.

An excerpt from *Heidi Heckelbeck and the Lost Library [...]*